**Roy Apps**

# THE TWITCHES

*Illustrated by Carla Daly*

POMEGRANATE · PRESS ·

Text copyright © 2008 Roy Apps
Illustrations copyright © 2008 Carla Daly

First published by Simon & Schuster Young Books

This edition published by Pomegranate Press
Dolphin House, 51 St Nicholas Lane, Lewes, Sussex BN7 2JZ
www.pomegranate-press.co.uk

ISBN 978-0-954-89759-8

British Library cataloguing-in-publication data
A catalogue record for this book is available from the British
Library

Printed and bound in England by 4edge Ltd, Hockley, Essex.

"Slithering snail's slime!" said Gert. "Look at this, Lil! In *The Daily Spellegraph*!"

Lil snatched the morning paper from her.

"Mmmm . . . Warm Spells . . ." she read. "What's that – a new kind of curse?"

"No! That's the weather forecast, you *angel*!" replied Gert.

Now Gert said "you angel", because she and Lil were witches and "angel" is just about the rudest thing you can call a witch. It's as bad as calling your sister's boyfriend "spotty-nose", or your teacher "wally-face".

"I mean," said Gert, "look at our horoscope."

Gert and Lil were twins as well as witches, and the proper name for twins who are also witches is, of course, *twitches*.

Lil screwed up her bony face and this is what she
read: *"You will find happiness, contentment and lots and
lots of money if you put your old life behind you and make
a brand new start."*

"Huh! What a load of old hoo-ha," Lil snorted.
"How can we put our old life behind us and make a
brand new start! At our age?"

"Why not at our age? I think that a hundred-and-thirteen-and-a-quarter is a very good age for twitches to put their old life behind them and make a new start," muttered Gert.

Lil stroked her bony chin with a long, craggy finger and looked at Madame Bestingo's horoscope again. From between her black and yellow teeth, she let out a long, drawn-out sigh.

"I'll tell you something," she said. "I certainly could do with a bit of happiness, contentment and lots and lots of money."

And this was certainly very true. For although Gert and Lil had been witching for a long time, they were not very good at it. In fact, they were terrible.

They had only ever once composed a Really Evil Magic Curse. It went:

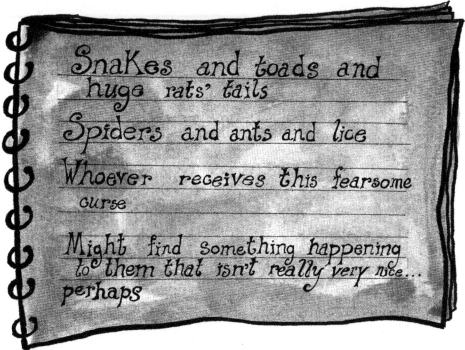

Snakes and toads and huge rats' tails
Spiders and ants and lice
Whoever receives this fearsome curse
Might find something happening to them that isn't really very nice... perhaps

But it had never worked.

They had only ever once composed a Really Evil Magic Potion. It was called "Limp Lizard Leg and Squashed Beetle Cocktail".

But it had never worked.

LIMP Lizard and Squashed Beetle Cocktail

Gert and Lil went outside and took down the sign hanging over their front door which read:

21 Gert and Lil Twitches. 21
curses, potions and spells
to suit every pocket.

They gave each of their thirteen
copper cauldrons a thorough
scrub and put them
up in the attic
out of the way.

Then, for the first time in twenty-seven years, Lil cleaned her teeth and for the first time in thirty-four years, Gert had a bath.

"Right then," said Lil. "That's that. Our old life is behind us and we've made a brand new start. Now all we have to do is to sit back and wait for contentment, happiness and lots and lots of money to be ours."

So they sat back and waited.

And waited.

For five whole shivering, witching minutes Gert and Lil sat waiting, hunched up over their damp, smokey fire. They glared and glowered at each other and, in general, looked very sour indeed.

"Well, do you *feel* happy and contented and rich for having given up witching and made a brand new start?" snarled Lil.

"Do I *look* happy and contented and rich?" snapped back Gert. And she ground both of her black teeth together.

"Almost," snorted Lil.

"Almost?" Gert's brow cracked into tiny wrinkles.

"Yes, you're not so much happy and rich as *snappy* and *witch*!" shrieked Lil. And she threw back her head, kicked her bony feet in the air and cackled with laughter at her wonderful wit. Because Lil thought her jokes were really witty. But, of course, just like her potions, her curses and her breath, they were *terrible*.

"Oh, curse that Madame Bestingo and her stupid horoscope," hissed Gert.

Lil stopped her cackling. "Now *that's* a good idea!" she said.

"What is?"

"Cursing Madame Bestingo! Let's go and give her a right old curse. That'll show her."

Gert's craggy face lit up with a toothy grin.

They found Madame Zsa Zsa Bestingo's address in the 'phone book under "A" for Astrologers. Then they put on their tall black hats and set off to give her a right old curse.

# Chapter Two

Madam Zsa Zsa Bestingo's office was in the town
centre above Jules' Hairdressing Salon. Gert and Lil
opened the door and found themselves face-to-face
with a nervous little man who peered at them
through gold-rimmed spectacles.

"We are looking for Madame Zsa Zsa Bestingo,"
Gert demanded. The man smiled back weakly.

"Then, dear ladies, look no further," he said. "For I am she."

Gert gulped so that her adam's apple slid all the way down her scrawny neck and back up again. "But you're a *man*!"

"Madame Zsa Zsa Bestingo is my professional name," explained the man. "My real name is Cecil Blenkinsop."

"That's the least of your problems," butted in Lil. She pulled out a copy of *The Daily Spellegraph*. "See this? Both my sister and I have made a brand new start, but we haven't found happiness, contentment–"

"Or lots and lots of money," Gert interrupted.

Gert and Lil bent close to Cecil Blenkinsop.
"Snakes and toads and huge rats' tails . . ." they
began to chant.

"Pardon?" asked Cecil Blenkinsop, politely.
"It's a curse!" hissed Lil.

Cecil Blenkinsop squeaked in terror, then leapt from his desk like a frog that has sat on a firework. He made a dash for the door and half-ran, half-fell down the stairs into Jules' Hairdressing Salon. Gert and Lil followed in hot pursuit.

Suddenly, Cecil
Blenkinsop turned and
faced the twitches.
"B-b-b-but cursing *me*
won't give *you*
happiness, contentment
or lots and lots of
money, will it?"

"Er . . . no . . ." Lil agreed, thoughtfully. "That is
true . . ."

"Then let's see how we can solve your problem," continued Cecil Blenkinsop, becoming more and more brave by the second. "What exactly did you make your brand new start *doing*?"

"Doing?" frowned Lil, puzzled.

"My dear ladies, making a new start must involve *doing* something! Something that is useful and helpful to other people."

"Urgh," said Lil.

"Yuk," said Gert.

Then Gert noticed a sign by the door:

"That would be a useful thing to do – helping customers look smart and glamorous and young, wouldn't it, Cecil?" asked Gert.

Cecil Blenkinsop nodded.

"And if we become Hairdressing Assistants, happiness and contentment will be ours . . ."

"And lots and lots of money," added Gert.

"Cecil, the cursing is off," announced Lil. "Take us to see Jules the Hairdresser, instead."

"Ladies, you need go no further, for I am he," Cecil smiled thinly. "It so happens, that as well as being Madame Zsa Zsa Bestingo the Astrologer, I am also Jules, owner of Jules' Hairdressing Salon."

# Chapter Three

Gert and Lil's first customer was none other than
Councillor Mrs Anthea Atkinson-Smythe.

"Shampoo and set, please," she sniffed. "And
could you touch up my highlights, please."

Lil spun Councillor Mrs Anthea Atkinson-Smythe round in her chair, and the fourth time round, caught hold of her head, shoved it into the bowl and whisked on the tap.

"Oooooh!" squeaked Councillor Mrs Anthea Atkinson-Smythe.

"Cold enough for you, is it dear?" asked Lil, in a sweet voice.

"*B-r-r-r-e-o-w!*" shivered Councillor Mrs Anthea Atkinson-Smythe.

"It'll help keep your skin nice and rough and crinkly," explained Lil. For she always used icy water when she washed — which, of course, wasn't very often.

*SCRAPE*, went Gert's furious finger-nails along Councillor Mrs Anthea Atkinson-Smythe's scalp.

"*Eiikkk!*" went Councillor Mrs Anthea Atkinson-Smythe.

"I'm so h-a-p-p-y," sang Gert as she tipped a few bottles of colouring over Councillor Mrs Anthea Atkinson-Smythe's hair.

"And I'm so c-o-n-t-e-n-t-e-d . . ." screeched Lil as she wound the curlers tightly into Councillor Mrs Anthea Atkinson-Smythe's hair.

Gert rammed the hair-dryer over Councillor Mrs Anthea Atkinson-Smythe's head.

"Ouch!" squawked Councillor Mrs Anthea Atkinson-Smythe.

"Lots and lots of money will soon be ours," cackled Gert to herself.

# Chapter Four

Half-an-hour later, Lil yanked the hair-dryer from
Councillor Mrs Anthea Atkinson-Smythe's head.

There was a moment's silence, then—

"*Aaaaarghhhhh!!!!!*" shrieked Councillor Mrs
Anthea Atkinson-Smythe.

And no wonder, because her hair was striped orange, mauve and lime-green. She looked like a punk parrot.

"You horrid, disgusting old hags!" she screamed at Gert and Lil.

Lil took this as a compliment. "We try to keep our customers satisfied," she beamed.

"Get rid of it!" screeched Councillor Mrs Anthea Atkinson-Smythe.

"Are you sure?" asked Gert in a puzzled voice.

"Get rid of it this instant!"

"Very well," sighed Gert. And she took a large pair of gleaming silver scissors from the shelf.

"No, I don't mean—" screamed Councillor Mrs Anthea Atkinson-Smythe, in a horrified panic.

But too late.

With one huge snip,
Gert cut off all of
Councillor Mrs Anthea
Atkinson-Smythe's hair.

"*Aaarrrggh!*" shrieked
Councillor Mrs Anthea
Atkinson-Smythe.

And no wonder, for her head was now as pink
and as bald as a baby's bottom.

All the shrieking and the screeching and the
screaming had brought Cecil Blenkinsop rushing
down the stairs. He took one look at Councillor Mrs
Anthea Atkinson-Smythe and turned as pale as
pastry.

"Out! Out of my Salon this instant!" he yelled at Gert and Lil.

Councillor Mrs Anthea Atkinson-Smythe sobbed like a fog-horn out of control.

Lil's eyes began to blaze like two hot coals. *"Snakes and toads and huge rats' tails,"* she hissed, dancing menacingly around Cecil.

*" . . . Spiders and ants and lice,*
*Whoever receives this fearsome curse*
*Might find something happening to them that isn't really*
*very nice*
*Perhaps."*

But nothing happened.

Suddenly Gert reached up her skirt and whisked out a bottle of Limp Lizard Leg and Squashed Beetle Cocktail.

"This'll turn you into a warty toad, Cecil Blenkinsop!" she roared. She sank both her teeth into the cork and pulled . . .

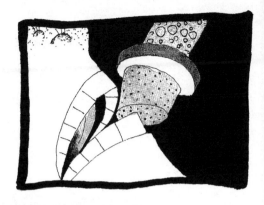

"Go steady, Gert!" warned Lil.

Whoosh! Plop! Splash!!!

One whole litre of Limp Lizard Leg and Squashed Beetle Cocktail shot out of the bottle and all over

Councillor Mrs Anthea Atkinson-Smythe's bald head.

"*Aaargh!*" she shrieked.

And then an extraordinary thing happened. Through the sticky liquid which was dripping off Councillor Mrs Anthea Atkinson-Smythe's scalp, something was beginning to sprout . . .

"Slithering snail's slime!" exclaimed Lil.

It wasn't snail's slime that was sprouting on Councillor Mrs Anthea Atkinson-Smythe's scalp, though, but a mass of shining blonde hair.

# Chapter Five

As Councillor Mrs Anthea Atkinson-Smythe walked out of Jules' Hairdressing Salon, her thick, golden curls glistened in the afternoon sun.

Cecil turned to Gert and Lil.

"My dear, dear ladies. Believe me, I can assure you that happiness, contentment and lots and lots of money will now be yours."

"About time too," said Lil.

"The labels will have to be changed, of course . . ."

"Changed?" asked Gert in a puzzled voice.

"Oh goodness me, yes. Limp Lizard Leg and Squashed Beetle Cocktail would never, never do. *Any suggestions for a new name?*"

"How about Limp Lizard Leg and Squashed Beetle *Hair Restorer?*" suggested Lil.

41

"I was thinking rather more of something like
MISSES GERTRUDE AND LILY'S LUXURIOUS AND
FRAGRANT HAIR RESTORING LOTION," said Cecil.

"Urgh!" said Gert.

"Yuk!" said Lil.

# Chapter Six

That same afternoon, Gert and Lil sold one hundred and eleven bottles of MISSES GERTRUDE AND LILY'S LUXURIOUS AND FRAGRANT HAIR RESTORING LOTION.

"Our Cecil's a very good astrologer," said Gert.

"Oh yes," agreed Lil. "I knew all along that happiness, contentment and lots and lots of money would be ours once we had made a brand new start." She paused, and then added, "But I didn't realize it was going to be quite so *hair-raising!*"

She and Gert cackled long and loud.

And no wonder, for it was one of Lil's very *worst* jokes.

# Roy Apps

# the tWITCHES on HORRIDAY

*Illustrated by Carla Daly*

Text copyright © 2008 Roy Apps
Illustrations copyright © 2008 Carla Daly

First published by Simon & Schuster Young Books

This edition published by Pomegranate Press
Dolphin House, 51 St Nicholas Lane, Lewes, Sussex BN7 2JZ
www.pomegranate-press.co.uk

ISBN 978-0-954-89759-8

British Library cataloguing-in-publication data
A catalogue record for this book is available from the British
Library

Printed and bound in England by 4edge Ltd, Hockley, Essex.

# CHAPTER ONE

"Come to Gertie-Wertie, little warty toad . . ." Gert put on her sweetest, softest voice, but it still came out like a cackle of an old crow.

This was hardly surprising, because she and her twin sister Lil were twitches, that is, they were *twins* who were also *witches*.

They were crawling on their scrawny hands and knobbly knees through their overgrown garden, hunting for a nice, fat, juicy, warty toad for supper.

"Don't know why you can't make do with tinned toad," muttered Lil.

"Because *I* have *taste*, crab-face," snorted Gert.

"Croak!" came a sound like a enormous burp.

"Manners Gert, please," snapped Lil.

"That wasn't me, you old twitch!" hissed Gert.

"Croak!"

A great big warty toad sprang out from under a
dock leaf.

"There he goes, Lil!"

Crashing through the bindweed and brambles
they went, the warty toad leaping from left to right,
a few paces in front of them.

With one extra long bound it leapt right over the
hedge and out of the garden.

With one extra long bound Gert and Lil leapt right
over the hedge after it and –

"Aaaargh!!!!!"

*Thump.*

"Yeoww!!!"

– landed straight on the back of a passing lorry.

But not just any old passing lorry. For when Gert and Lil finished rubbing their bruises they looked round and saw that with them were a Roman general, four Martians, two pirates and Count Dracula.

The lorry turned into the recreation ground and
screeched to halt by a big marquee.

"Curse this lorry!" fumed Lil.

"Good idea," agreed Gert. "Let's turn all the petrol
into bat's blood!"

Suddenly, a very large, fat man wearing a
glittering gold chain around his neck clambered on
to the back of the lorry.

"It's the Mayor!" gasped Gert.

And so it was. He was followed by a short, fat little
man in a grey suit. The Mayor looked from the
Martians to the pirates to the Roman general to
Count Dracula and then his eyes finally rested on
Gert and Lil.

"Oh yes, oh yes, oh yes, oh yes," he said, and turning to the short, fat man in the grey suit added, "the witches are far and away the best."

The short, fat man wriggled and looked extremely uncomfortable. "Are you sure, your Worship?" he whispered anxiously to the Mayor. "I don't like the look of them one bit. How about that Count Dracula, he seems a nice lad?"

"Rubbish, Herbert," chortled the Mayor. And without further ado, he cleared his throat and announced: "As Mayor of this town, it is my great privilege to award first prize in this year's Summer Carnival Fancy Dress competition to the witches!" And he pinned a bright red rosette on Gert and Lil's black hats.

"You *twerp*," cackled Lil, "we haven't entered any comp– *Yeowww*!" she yelled as Gert kicked the boniest part of her very bony ankle.

"Er . . . What *is* the prize?" asked Gert with a glint in her greedy eye. "Is it lots and lots of money?"

"Oh no," said the Mayor. "It's an all expenses paid, fortnight's holiday in Spain, with Mr Herbert Sherbert here," – and he patted the short, fat little man on the head – "of Sherbert's Happy Holidays Limited. You will be staying at the magnificent Hotel Magnifico, owned by Mr Sherbert's cousin, Senor Alphonso Sherberto."

"Wow! Yuk!" beamed Gert.

"Phew! Putrid!" grinned Lil.

For these are witches' ways of saying that the idea of two weeks in Spain was a very attractive one indeed.

"I don't like the look of them, your Worship," hissed Herbert Sherbert.

"You're not meant to like the look of them! They're in Fancy Dress. Aren't you?" the Mayor asked Lil.

"Well," replied Lil doubtfully, "this is certainly a dress, but I'd hardly call it *fancy*,"

"Can you get warty toads in Spain?" asked Gert brightly.

And Herbert Sherbert turned as green as a lizard's leg.

# CHAPTER THREE

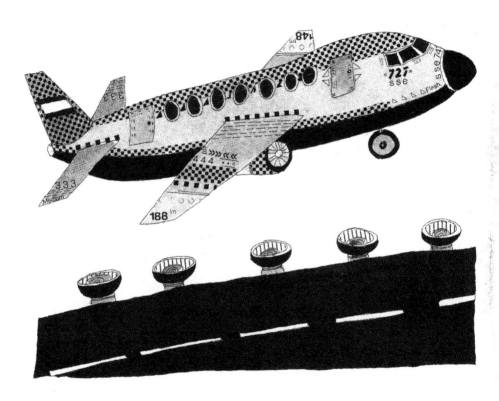

"Fasten your seat belts, we are about to land," crackled the Captain's voice over the loudspeaker.

The plane's tyres screeched as they hit the runway.

"Ooo-er, my ears have gone all funny," said Lil.

"They haven't *gone* all funny, they've always looked like that!" Gert laughed like an old hen with a megaphone.

All the passengers in the plane looked round to see what the dreadful noise was, while Herbert Sherbert slid further and further down his seat, trying to make himself invisible. "I told the Mayor they'd be trouble!" he muttered to himself.

Gert and Lil sat in the bus that was taking them
from the airport to the Hotel Magnifico.

"Slithering frog's spawn, it *is* hot, isn't Lil?"
exclaimed Gert.

And she took off her hat.

"Atchoo! Atchooo! Atchoooo!"

Immediately everybody on the bus started coughing and sneezing, for under Gert's hat were thirty six years' worth of dandruff, dust and cobwebs.

"*A-a-a-atch-o-o-o-o*!!!" went Lil.

"Why curse you, dear," cackled Gert, which is what witches say to each other when they sneeze.

Lil pulled the headrest cover off the seat in front and blew her nose into it – "*Paaaarpppp!*" – so loudly that the whole bus shook.

Everyone on the bus looked in horror at the twitches. Then they shot angry glances at Herbert Sherbert as if to say, "So, those disgusting old witches are with *you*, are they?"

And, of course, they were.

"Ah Herbert, welcome to the Hotel Magnifico!"
Senor Alphonso hugged his cousin until Herbert
felt that all his breath had been squeezed out of him.

"And you ladies must be the Fancy Dress
Competition winners!"
Senor Alphonso's smile
was so broad that his
gold-capped teeth
sparkled in the sun.

"How dare you, young man!" snarled Lil.

"Pardon?" exclaimed Senor Alphonso.

"Never in all my one hundred and thirteen and a quarter years have I been so insulted!" Lil went on. "Has no one ever taught you how to address your elders and betters?"

Now, it is very rude to call a witch a "lady". They much prefer it if you refer to them as "You Old Hag", or, if they are very important witches, "My Most Ancient Crone".

"Kindly address my sister and me as 'Madam Twitches'," she said, huffily. "Otherwise I'll curdle your blood into goat's yoghurt!"

"Er . . . of course, er . . . Madam Twitches," said Senor Alphonso, a little nervously. "They'd better not be any trouble!" he muttered under his breath to his cousin.

"You know, Gert, this looks a really scrummy menu," said Lil, as she and Gert sat down to dinner in the Hotel Magnifico's posh restaurant.

This is what the menu said:

MENU

for firsts

Toad-in-the-hole

for seconds

Mousse

"Senor Alphonso!" squawked Lil when her first course arrived. "What is *this*?" She prodded her toad-in-the-hole with a long and very grubby fingernail.

"Toad-in-the-hole."

"Well, I can't see any toad," complained Lil angrily.

A number of the other diners began to turn green and to look very ill indeed.

"And neither can I," added Gert. "What's this long round thing – it's not a slice of boiled snake is it?"

"That," said Senor Alphonso, shaking with anger, "is a sausage!"

"Then why does it say *toad* on your menu?" asked Lil. "My sister and I were looking forward to a nice fat, juicy, warty toad!"

"And another thing, young man!" boomed Gert.

Everyone turned round and Senor Alphonso froze on the spot.

"This *For Seconds*," Gert pointed to the menu, "is it dormouse or harvest mouse?"

Two ladies dining in the far corner screamed. And two gentlemen in the opposite corner fainted.

"It's not *mouse*!" yelled Senor Alphonso indignantly. "It's *mousse*! Strawberry mousse!"

"In that case," said Gert, acidly, "I'll just have a drink."

"A drink of what?" asked Senor Alphonso with a tremor.

"Oh, a small glass of slime juice will do," said Gert.

Several of the other diners rushed out clutching table napkins to their mouths.

"You . . . you disgusting old hags!" screamed Senor Alphonso in fury.

"Ah, you see, he likes us really," said Lil, with a black-toothed smile.

"Herbert!" snarled Senor Alphonso in his cousin's ear, "I want them out of my hotel and on the plane home, first thing in the morning!"

"That was the most uncomfortable night I have ever spent in my life," said Lil grumpily next morning. "Those sheets had been *washed*, you know, I'm sure of it!"

"Urgh! I'll be glad to get back home to the hovel," said Gert. "That strange smell, what was it?"

"Soap, I think," said Lil, with great disgust.

There was a knock at the door and in came a

chambermaid, loaded with dusters, brushes and a vacuum cleaner. "Good morning, I've come to clean your room," she said brightly.

Gert and Lil screwed up their faces in horror. "Language, please!" said Lil, in a shocked voice.

Suddenly, Gert's face broke out into a wide, toothless smile. "Have you got a spare broom?" she asked the chambermaid.

"We don't use brooms any more," replied the chambermaid, "we use this." She pointed to the vacuum cleaner. "It's a Whizzo Zoom."

"I thought we might as well take a trip before we go home," explained Gert to Lil, in a whisper. "See a bit of the countryside – we might even come across a warty toad or two."

"What, on this?" Lil eyed the Whizzo Zoom suspiciously.

"Why not? It's got a long handle, the same as a broomstick. Hop on."

*Whooosh*!

"Hey! Come back!" yelled the chambermaid.

But off went the Whizzo Zoom, with Gert and Lil clutching on to the handle.

*Crash*! went the potted fern on the landing, as they caught it a glancing blow.

"It's quite smooth, but not fast enough for my liking!" yelled Lil above the roar of the Whizzo Zoom.

"Left here," yelled Gert, as they reached the dining room door. And she put out her hand to signal.

*Crash!* went a full set of plates, bowls, cups and saucers as Gert's outstretched arm swept them off the crockery trolley.

On to the verandah they roared.

"Stop! You vandals! Stop!" screamed Senor
Alphonso, but Gert and Lil had no idea how to stop
the Whizzo Zoom.

Senor Alphonso stepped backwards as the Whizzo
Zoom hurtled towards him.

"Oo-er!" cried Lil, as she suddenly saw the hotel swimming pool in front of them.

*Splash*!

"Aaaaargh!" cried Senor Alphonso.

*Splash*!

"Glug . . . Glug . . ." went Gert.

"Glug . . . Glug . . ." went Lil.

"You . . .!" spluttered Senor Alphonso, as they all bobbed up to the surface.

"Just thought, we'd *drop in*!" cackled Gert, opening her mouth wide in a loud, toothless laugh. For Gert's jokes, like her manners and her taste in warty toads, were really, really bad.

"I told the Mayor they'd be trouble!" explained Herbert Sherbert to his cousin, as he came racing across to the swimming pool.

"Get them a plane home now!"

"I can't, Alphonso!"

"Can't? What do you mean can't?"

"The next plane doesn't leave until tomorrow!"

"I'm not having you anywhere *near* my hotel!"
fumed a very wet Senor Alphonso. "You will stay
the night over there."

He led Gert and Lil out of the hotel courtyard and
across a field.

"And you, Herbert," he called over his shoulder to
his cousin, "you will pay for all the damage they
have done to my hotel!"

They arrived at a crumbling, tumbling-down old shed. "This is all *you're* fit for," said Senor Alphonso crossly. "It's where I used to keep my goats."

"Mmmmm, yes, so I can smell," sniffed Lil.

"Mmmmm, what a stink," sniffed Gert, happily. "This is more like it."

Herbert Sherbert gulped like a man who has
swallowed a bag of marbles. "You *like* it in here?"

"Not half," said Gert, hugging herself. "It feels
so . . . so *damp*. And *so* filthy!"

"And it looks as if there are plenty of spiders and
cockroaches about," put in Lil. "Just you wait until
we tell them all back home down at *The Hag's Head*."

"You mean . . . your friends would want to come and stay in my old goat house for their holidays?" asked Alphonso, doubtfully.

"Not holidays. Witches don't have holidays. They have *horrid*ays," explained Gert.

"'Sherbert's Hideous Horridays'. Mmmmm, I like it," mused Herbert.

"If the Twitches find the customers and I organize the travel . . . your goat shed could be fully booked all year round, Alphonso."

Senor Alphonso thought long and hard.
"Mmmmm, I wouldn't have to decorate. I wouldn't
have to pay a chambermaid to clean. There would be
no laundry bills. It wouldn't cost me *anything*!" he
exclaimed.

"You would have to let us have two weeks'
horriday a year, here, free," said Gert.

"And you would have to forget about charging me
for the damage the twitches did to the Hotel
Magnifico," added Herbert.

"Of course! Of course!" said Senor Alphonso,
beaming his best hotel manager's smile once again.

"What a good thing it was you two ladies er . . .
Madam Twitches who won the Fancy Dress
Competition."

"Exactly what I told the Mayor," said Herbert,
with his fingers crossed firmly behind his back.

That night in the goat's shed, Gert woke Lil with a start.

"Can you hear what I can hear?" she said.

*Croak!*

"A warty toad!" exclaimed Lil. "A nice, fat, juicy, warty toad! Where is it?"

"I can't see! It's dark."

"I think it's over there in the corner. Are you ready to pounce? After two, right?"

"Right."

"One. Two . . ."

AAAAAARRRRRGGGGGHHHHH!!!!!